Nosy Rosie

Holly Keller

Greenwillow Books
An Imprint of HarperCollinsPublishers

For Isabel

Nosy Rosie
Copyright © 2006 by Holly Keller
All rights reserved. Manufactured in China.
www.harpercollinschildrens.com

Watercolor and black line were used
to prepare the full-color art.
The text type is Veljovic.

Library of Congress Cataloging-in-Publication Data
Keller, Holly.
Nosy Rosie / by Holly Keller.
"Greenwillow Books."
p. cm.
Summary: Rosie the fox's excellent sense of smell is
good for finding things, but she stops using it after
everyone begins to call her "Nosy Rosie."
ISBN-10: 0-06-078758-9 (trade bdg.)
ISBN-13: 978-0-06-078758-5 (trade bdg.)
ISBN-10: 0-06-078759-7 (lib. bdg.)
ISBN-13: 978-0-06-078759-2 (lib. bdg.)
[1. Names, Personal—Fiction. 2. Smell—Fiction.
3. Senses and sensation—Fiction. 4. Foxes—Fiction.
5. Animals—Fiction.] I. Title.
PZ7.K28132Nos 2006 [E]—dc22 2005022183

First Edition 10 9 8 7 6 5 4 3 2 1

GREENWILLOW BOOKS

"Here's your lost cookie," Rose said to Truffles.

"How did you find it?" Truffles asked.

"I smelled it," said Rose.

Rose could find anything with her nose.

She found Meadow's dress-up lipstick
when it fell out of her pocket.
"It smells red," said Rose.

She found Spike's new baseball
when he lost it in the grass.
"It smells new," Rose explained.

She found baby Harry's bottle
when he put it in the mailbox.
"I know the smell of milk,"
Rose said.

And when Mama couldn't find her handkerchief,
Rose found it because it smelled like Mama.

One day Meadow called Rose
Nosy Rosie.
The name stuck
and everyone started calling her
Nosy Rosie.

Rose hated it.
"Don't call me that," she said,
but nobody listened.
So Rose stopped finding things.

"Please, Nosy Rosie," Meadow said
when she couldn't find her jump rope.
Rose pretended not to hear.

"Please, Nosy Rosie," said Truffles
when her doll's dress
was missing.

"Please, Nosy Rosie," said Spike
when he lost his baseball again.
Rose walked away.

"I don't hear you because that's *not* my name,"
Rose shouted.

"We don't need you, anyway," said Truffles.

"We can find our own things," said Meadow.

"Fine with me," said Rose, and she went outside.

Rose walked in the forest behind the house,

because she loved the smell of pine trees.

After a while she stopped to rest.

When she woke up,
the sun was fading.
Rose sniffed the air.
Then she sniffed the ground.
She smelled powder and soap.

Rose knew right away that she smelled baby Harry.

She followed

her nose

to a thorny bush,

and there was Harry trapped underneath it.

He was very happy to see Rose.

Rose untangled him and smoothed his fur.

"I was looking for you," said Harry.

When Mama discovered that Harry was missing,
she was frantic. She told everyone to search for him.

Meadow looked under things,

Spike looked into things,

Truffles looked behind things,

and Mama looked everywhere else.

"We need Nosy Rosie," said Truffles.

"She could find Harry in two minutes," said Meadow.

"Where *is* Nosy Rosie?" Spike asked.

"I haven't seen her for hours."

"Oh, dear," said Mama.

Rose and Harry got home a few minutes later.

"I smelled him in the bushes," said Rose.

Mama hugged them both.

"You're awesome," said Meadow.

"You're amazing," said Truffles.

"You're incredible," said Spike.

"Thank you," said Rose,

"but I'm just Rose,

and that's the only name I want."

And nobody ever called her anything else again.